DATE DUE

MAY 2 1 ꞵꞵꞵ			

MOUTH MOTHS MORE CLASSROOM TALES

Mouth Moths

More Classroom Tales

Douglas Evans

PICTURES BY
Larry Di Fiori

FRONT STREET
Asheville, North Carolina

Library of Congress Cataloging-in-Publication Data
Evans, Douglas.
Mouth moths : and more classroom tales / Douglas Evans;
pictures by Larry Di Fiori.—1st ed.
p. cm.
Summary: At W.T. Melon Elementary School, in the tall teacher's
classroom, mysterious events continue to happen, from mouth moths
and tattle-tale alarms, to bucking bronco chairs.
ISBN-13: 978-1-932425-23-9
(hardcover : alk. paper)
[1. Schools—Fiction. 2. Magic—Fiction. 3. Behavior—Fiction.]
I. Di Fiori, Lawrence, ill. II. Title.
PZ7.E8775Mo 2006
[Fic]—dc22
2006000797

FRONT STREET
An Imprint of Boyds Mills Press, Inc.
A Highlights Company

815 Church Street
Honesdale, Pennsylvania 18431

For the students at The Academy

Contents

The Doghouse

RAISE YOUR HAND TO TALK
KEEP YOUR HANDS TO YOURSELF
STAY IN YOUR SEAT
USE A SOFT VOICE

Four rules were posted above the blackboard in the classroom at the end of the hall at W. T. Melon Elementary School. In the corner of the blackboard, the tall teacher was drawing a doghouse with chalk.

After completing the peaked roof, he turned toward his class of third-graders. "If you break a classroom rule, your name goes into the doghouse," he explained. "That's a warning. Break a rule again and I put a check mark by your name. That will cost you five minutes of recess. Another broken rule, another check mark, another five minutes of recess lost. Any questions?"

The tall teacher studied his new students. On this first day of school, they wore looks of excitement mixed with concern mixed with curiosity.

"What if we get a hundred check marks by our name?" asked Matthew in the second row.

"Do the math, Matthew," said the teacher. "Five minutes

times one hundred. That's a lot of missed recesses."

Hannah, who sat in the fourth row, raised her hand. "Can we still hug each other?" she asked.

"Hands to yourself means hands to yourself, Hannah," said the teacher. "You can hug all you want on the playground."

From the third row, Alex called loudly, "But I can't remember all those rules."

"The rules will remain posted above the blackboard all year, Alex," said the tall teacher. "And don't forget the fourth one. Keep your voice down."

"How can I go to the boys' room if I have to stay in my seat?" said Zachary from his back-row chair.

The third-graders giggled, and the teacher's ears glowed pink. He called on Loren, who had her hand raised.

"Do we have to take many tests this year?" Loren asked.

Miss Nosewiggle, a guinea pig with orange fur, stirred in her cage on the science shelf.

"We'll talk about testing later, Loren," said the teacher. "Now, does everyone know what the expression *in the doghouse* means?"

"It means you're in trouble," Paul blurted out from the second row. "My mom's always telling my dad he's in the doghouse."

"That's correct, Paul," said the teacher. "But don't forget to raise your hand if you want to talk. Now, class, I think that's enough questions, and we'll begin our morning.

Just be careful to follow the classroom rules throughout third grade so you can stay out of the doghouse. I know we're going to have a great school year together."

Mouth Moths

The tall teacher leaned against the black-board. "Now, class, take out your phonics books and pencils."

The rows of desktops opened.

Crack! Crack!

The desktops came down.

Smack! Smack!

The workbooks landed on the hard surfaces.

The teacher was about to give further instructions when a voice blared from the second row.

"What page?"

The words came from a skinny boy with curly black hair. He was batting the cover of his phonics book back and forth between his hands.

The tall teacher turned toward the blackboard. Inside the doghouse he wrote *Paul*.

"That's your warning, Paul," he said. "Remember, raise your hand if you want to ask a question."

Next, the teacher wrote *AW* and *AU* on the blackboard. "Who can tell me what sound these letters make?"

Twenty-four hands went up. Only Paul opened his mouth. Out came the call Tarzan makes while swinging through the jungle. "AWW-A-AWWWW-A-AWWWWW!"

The teacher spun around. He dashed off a check mark next to Paul's name in the doghouse.

"You just lost five minutes of recess, Paul!" he said. "Raise your hand before you speak."

"Awww," said Paul.

The teacher took a deep breath before continuing. "Now, class, who can give me a word with the *aw* sound in it?"

Again a forest of hands rose into the air. But before anyone could answer, the curly-haired boy in the second row called out, "Paul! My name says *awwww*. Pauuuuul!"

The students sat in silent suspense. The tall teacher's ears were red, a sure sign that he was boiling mad.

"Your second check mark, Paul!" he said through his teeth. "Stop interrupting! Give others a turn! Now, ah, who knows a word with the *aw* sound?"

One by one the students who had a hand raised were called on, and one by one they answered.

"Author!"

"Law!"

"Daughter!"

"Creepy crawler!"

"Moths!" shouted Paul. He was waving a hand in front of his face.

The tall teacher frowned. "Yes, Paul, *moths* says *aw*, but with an *O*, not with *A-W* or *A-U*. And I said raise your hand, not flap it in front of you."

But Paul hadn't been answering or even paying attention to his teacher. He was trying to catch three small moths that were fluttering before his face like pieces of confetti. Each was the size of a thumbnail and had pink wings. The moths moved in quick *O*'s and *V*'s no more than three inches in front of him.

"They came out of my mouth!" Paul told himself. "I saw them fly out! One, two, three! The moths shot from my mouth the last time I opened it!"

While Paul continued waving, the class continued calling out *A-W* and *A-U* words. Apparently, no one else saw the flittering creatures.

"Yawn!"

"Jawbreaker!"

"Caution!"

"Australia!"

"This is awful!" Paul cried. And the instant his lips parted, three more moths flew straight out of his mouth.

Paul went cross-eyed trying to watch the small pink swirling W's. When he waved both hands, they scattered in six directions. Just a few feet away, they were nearly invisible. But they didn't stay away long. Soon they were back, orbiting his head again as if it were a light bulb.

"Fifteen minutes, Paul," called the tall teacher, adding a third check mark next to his name in the doghouse.

"Awww!" said Paul, and out sailed another three moths.

Zigging and zagging, the pink things flew in a frenzy before Paul's face. Their batting wings tickled his eyelashes and eyebrows. They darted into his ears and fluttered against his neck. When they brushed his nostrils, he gave a huge sneeze—*Ahhhh-choo!*— and released three more.

"Time for recess, class," the teacher announced. "But Paul, you'll stay inside the entire time. What must I do to get you to raise your hand before talking?"

Watching a moth land on

the end of his nose, Paul only shrugged. He dared not open his mouth again.

After the class and the tall teacher had left the room, Paul sat watching the whirling moths. Blowing only sent them flitting in circles. Fanning them with his phonics book blew them outward. But within seconds they returned, fluttering faster than before.

Frustrated, Paul stood and paced the room. The pink cloud went with him. When he passed the computer, an idea struck.

"I'll check out these moths on the Internet," he told himself. "You can find anything on the Web."

With the moths still bombarding him, Paul tapped at the keyboard. A Google search turned up 323,000 sites about moths. Scrolling down, he found a site that looked promising: *North American Classroom Moths.* He clicked on the blue link and was soon viewing screen after screen of moth photos, each accompanied by a caption stating the moth's name and description.

"Coat Closet Moth," Paul read under a picture of a large moth with brown wings and a set of sharp teeth. "No, that's not the one. Cootie-Catcher Moth? Nope.

Math Moth? Uh-uh. Chalk Moth? Teacher Coffee Moth? *I don't think so.* How about the Writing Paper Moth? No, that's got white wings with blue stripes, and it nibbles holes in students' writing paper."

Paul continued scrolling down the computer screen until a small pink moth appeared. He studied first the image and then the moth that had just taken off from his chin.

"Aha!" he said. "It's a Mouth Moth."

The caption below the picture read:

Mouth Moth: Pink wings. One-half-inch wingspan. Visible only at short range. Lives in the Adam's apples of grade-school students. Can come out in classrooms when certain sounds of the letter A, such as aw *and* ah, *are spoken. When inspecting throats, doctors ask children to say "Ahh" so that they can check for Mouth Moths.*

"Awesome!" said Paul, allowing another trio of moths to fly off his tongue. "But how do I get rid of my Mouth Moths? They're driving me batty."

He scrolled down to a section called "Mouth Moth Treatment and Prevention." It said:

Unlike most moths, Mouth Moths avoid light. If Mouth Moths are driving you batty, keep your mouth open wide. Soon the moths will return to their nest in your Adam's apple.

To prevent Mouth Moths from escaping, apply pressure to

*your Adam's apple each time you speak out in class. Lifting
your arm above your head does this best.*

Paul heard voices at the door. His class was returning
from recess. Swatting at the moths, he shut down the
computer and returned to his seat in the second row. With
his head tilted back, he opened his mouth wide as if he
were in a dentist chair. In this position he waited.

Kimberly led the line of third-graders into the classroom. "Paul looks dead!" she said.

"Or else that's the world's longest yawn," said Zack,
staring at Paul.

Despite the taunts, Paul dared not move. A moth sat
on his lower lip. It tasted like a lemon drop as it stepped
across his tongue. His throat tickled as the moth slid
down toward his Adam's apple. Paul thought he might
gag, but no—the creature went down smoothly.

The tall teacher entered the classroom. He looked at
Paul still with his mouth agape and gave
an "at least he's quiet" shrug.

"OK, class, we'll continue with
phonics," he said. "Do page twenty-
three in your workbooks."

This was good news for Paul. He
could keep his mouth open and work
at the same time. As he wrote answers
in his workbook, the Mouth Moths
continued to land on his lower lip. He

breathed through his nose, for fear of blowing them away. One by one, the light, tasty things stepped onto his tongue and slid down to the lump in his throat. After the last one disappeared, he gnashed his teeth tightly together.

"What did that Internet site say?" Paul asked himself. "Oh, yes—to keep Mouth Moths from escaping, I must apply pressure to my Adam's apple before speaking."

Paul lifted his right arm above his head. He felt his chest lift and push against his throat.

The tall teacher looked up from his desk and nodded in approval.

"Can I go to the boys' room?" Paul asked. "I gotta go awwwfully bad."

Good—the arm trick worked. Not one pink moth shot from his mouth.

"Sure, Paul," said the teacher. "And I'm glad you remembered to raise your hand before talking out."

With his hand still up, Paul stood and stepped into the hallway. He walked down the hall, not daring to lower his arm.

By the boys' room door, Mr. Leeks, the custodian of W. T. Melon Elementary School, was leaning on his mop admiring the fall artwork taped to the wall. The janitor studied the boy. "Practicing to be the Statue of Liberty for Halloween, Paul?" he asked.

"Nope, I just don't want any more trouble with Mouth Moths," said Paul.

"That's good," Mr. Leeks said. And when Paul remained standing there with his hand up, he asked, "So do you have a question?"

Paul nodded toward the artwork. "Awwwsome auuu-tumn drawwwings," he said. "See, no moths! Now I know how to keep them in my Adam's apple. Whenever I want to talk in class, I'll make sure to raise my hand."

"That's good," said the janitor.

Keeping his hand in the air, Paul pushed open the boys' room door and stepped inside. A short time later the hallway filled with a triumphant call,
"AWW-A-AWWWW-A-
   AWWWWW!"

Spot

Myra   Oct 15

Writer's Workshop

Every Monday we have Writer's Workshop. It's called Writer's Workshop although we only write and work but never get to shop. We write in journals, except I'm a bad writer. That is because I don't ever have anything to write about. Our teacher said this story must be five sentences long.

The End

Myra sat in the third row in the classroom at the end of the hall. Her chin rested on an elbow that pressed upon the blue-lined paper that was stapled inside her Writer's Workshop journal that lay on her desktop.

The tall teacher stood behind Myra, shaking his head. "Not again, Myra," he said.

"*Every* Writer's Workshop you write about hating Writer's Workshop!"

21

"But I don't know what else to write about," Myra complained. "My mind goes blank when I see blank paper."

"Good writers write about things they've done," said the teacher. "They write about what they know."

"But I'm only eight years old," Myra reminded him. "Eight-year-olds have hardly done anything. Eight-year-olds hardly know anything."

"Write about what you did last weekend," the teacher suggested.

"I hardly did a thing," Myra griped. "I spent my whole Saturday morning in the emergency room because my brother stuck a Lego up his nose. After that I had soccer practice, ballet practice, piano practice, and karate practice. I hardly had time to do anything."

The tall teacher flipped to a blank page in Myra's journal. "Let's start writing, Myra," he said. "I'm sure you can think of a good topic."

"Hardly," said Myra.

Myra wrote her name and the date in the top margin of the paper. She put a small *X* in the middle where she thought five sentences would end.

"But I still don't know what to write about," she said.

Sometimes Myra thought best while staring at the ceiling. Tilting her head far back, she looked beyond the long fluorescent lights and focused on the white acoustic tiles that covered the top of her classroom. Each tile had hundreds of small holes in it.

"What could all those holes be for?" Myra asked herself. "I wonder how many holes are up there. Let's see—one, two, three, four, five . . ."

As Myra counted, a hole directly overhead started to blink. Could an ant be crawling out? Some ceiling bug? She squinted to see more clearly. No, oozing from the hole was a large black drop. For a second it hung on the hole. It wobbled and swayed before finally falling straight toward Myra's desk.

"My classroom's leaking," said Myra, watching the drop drip.

Halfway down the black drop flattened. It continued its descent, now floating like a flower petal. Inches above Myra's desktop, two thin legs sprouted from its bottom and two thin arms popped out its sides. On two thin feet it landed, right on the top margin of Myra's Writer's Workshop journal.

Myra leaned forward to take a good look. The flat black disc was running along the top blue-ruled line in her notebook while shouting in a thin, high voice, "See Spot! See Spot run!"

Myra wrinkled her nose and groaned. "Your name's Spot?" she asked.

"Run, Spot, run," said the thing, racing to the edge of her journal. As it did so, a page flipped over to the Writer's Workshop story Myra had just written. The black dot stood below the word *I'm*.

"What's going on?" Myra said. "What are you doing on my story?"

"*I'm* on the Spot," the thing called out.

Myra rubbed her eyeballs with her knuckles. "Whatever," she said.

After running some more, Spot lay under the word *That.*

"*That* hits the Spot!" it announced.

"That's weird," said Myra, looking around the room. No one else seemed to notice the big period racing around her journal.

At this point Spot sat on the word *about*. "There's a Spot on you," it said.

Myra groaned again.

Next, Spot hid behind the *x* in the word *except*. "Any guesses?" it asked.

Myra shrugged.

"*X* marks the Spot," came the answer.

The thing began moving again. "See Spot! See Spot run!"

Myra bent a finger and cocked it with her thumb. "Well, Spot," she said, holding her hand an inch from the black dot, "this paper will soon be Spot-less, because you're looking at my Spot remover. I have journal writing to do."

Spot waved its tiny arms. "Wait, Myra! Wait! You've hit a rough spot, and I can help."

Myra scowled. "*Hardly*. What good could you do?"

Spot walked over to the word *Myra* and sat down. "Being a third-grader, you should know how important spots are in writing," it said. "Without spots, sentences would never end. Can you write a question? And I'll bet you can't get excited! And think of all the letters a spot saves you when you use it at the end of an abbreviation. I could go on and on . . ."

"I see your point,"

said Myra, picking up her pencil. "Well, Spot, writing is a sore spot with me. And I'll be in a tight spot if I don't think of something to write about for Writer's Workshop."

"Then this is the right spot for me," said Spot.

At that moment Myra felt a hand on her shoulder. "Myra, who are you talking to?" The tall teacher stood behind her.

"Spot," the girl said. But a quick glance toward her paper told her that the dot had disappeared. She noticed, however, a fresh period after *Oct.*

The tall teacher frowned. "Well, Myra, I see only your old Writer's Workshop story. And you'll stay glued to that spot until you write something new."

After the teacher left, Myra tapped her journal with her pencil. "All right, Spot. Come on out. You said you could help me."

The period after *Oct* began to grow. A moment later Spot stood again on the paper.

"First, a quick spot check, Myra," it said. "Tell me your problem."

"I can't think of anything to write about," Myra said.

Spot paced back and forth along the top blue line. "Does your brain seemed blocked like a clogged drain?" it said.

"Uh-huh," said Myra.

"And does your writing hand freeze when you try to write?"

"Exactly."

Spot stopped on the word *Writer's*. "Myra, I believe . . . no, it's more than that—I'm *certain* that you suffer from a disorder that even the greatest writers on earth sometimes suffer from. Writer's block."

"Writer's block?" Myra said. "I have writer's block?"

"You see, Myra, your brain is filled with ideas," Spot explained. "There is a drain in the brain, a brain drain, that lets these ideas flow down your arm to your writing hand. For reasons teachers have never figured out, this brain drain at times gets clogged. Now hold up a pencil."

Myra held up her pencil with her left hand.

"Ah, a *southpaw!*" Spot exclaimed. "You're one of the rare left-handed writers—one in ten. That means that the drain to your left hand is blocked. With no way of getting out, your thoughts are just swirling around in your head, like water in a washing machine."

Myra stared at her journal. "Well, Spot, you might be able to help me end sentences and abbreviations, but I don't see how you can help me with writer's block."

Spot raced to the edge of Myra's desktop. "I'll be right back," it said. "Spotlight, please!"

Like a party balloon, Spot floated upward. The black dot sailed over to the shelf where the rainy-day games and toys were stored. A moment later a wooden block dropped off the shelf. Spot pushed the cube across the floor to Myra's desk.

"But that's just a plain old building block," Myra said, lifting the cube along with Spot onto her desktop.

"Not just a block, Myra, a left-handed *Writer's Unblock*," said Spot. "See the button. That's the hot spot. Go ahead. Press it."

With her pointer finger Myra pressed the black button in a corner of the cube. All at once the sides of the Writer's Unblock became transparent, as clear as plastic. In its center a small white tornado was swirling.

"Look closely, Myra," said Spot. "What do you spot?"

Resting her chin on her fist, Myra watched the tiny funnel cloud. At its bottom tip an image appeared.

"That's me," she said. "I see me as I was this morning standing by my bed in my pj's."

Spot paced the blue line again. "What else do you spot?"

Myra peered into the Writer's Unblock again.

"Oh, that was me when I was putting on my socks," she said. "I couldn't decide whether to wear red socks or blue socks, so I put on one of each."

As she spoke, a gurgling sound started churning inside her head. From deep within her brain came the glugging, slurping, and slish-sloshing sound of water going down a drain.

The scene inside the Writer's Unblock suddenly switched. At the base of the whirling cloud, Myra now saw herself eating breakfast, her favorite cereal concoction of Cheerios mixed with Lucky Charms mixed with Cap'n Crunch.

Switch!

She saw herself fighting with her brother.

Switch!

She was under her bed, searching for her homework.

Switch!

She was fighting with her brother again.

Switch!

She was studying her spelling list while brushing her teeth.

All the while the brain gurgling continued.

"You know, Spot," she said, "when I watch my morning like this, it doesn't seem so boring."

"Any day is the stuff for a good story," said Spot. "And here comes the high spot!"

Now Myra saw herself leaving her house. On the way out the door, *whack!*, her backpack banged on the door frame.

"There went my science fair experiment," she said. "A jar filled with an egg and vinegar. Phew!"

Glug, glug! went the sound in Myra's brain. *Gurgle, gurgle, glug!*

Before Myra knew it, she had a pencil in her hand. In her journal she wrote:

Myra   *Oct. 15*

Morning Disaster
My backpack smells like a salad bar. Here's why.

"Wait until you read what happened on my way to school, Spot," Myra said. "I hardly have enough room to write it all down."

"Your ideas were there all along, Myra, right on the spot," said Spot.

As Myra wrote, Spot pushed the block, which had turned back into wood, onto the floor.

"And now that your brain drain is flowing again, I have work to do elsewhere," it said. "Zack needs me after *Mr.* in his first paragraph, and Kimberly forgot me above all four *i*'s in the word *Mississippi*. And I know I'll find many parking spots in Hannah's journal. She's always careless with spelling, capitals, and punctuation. See Spot! See Spot run!"

But Myra didn't hear any of that. She was too busy writing.

Cuts

"No cuts!" Hannah shouted.

"Teacher! Kimberly took cuts!" called Paul.

"Kimberly cut me!" Myra complained.

"Stop taking cuts, Kimberly," snapped Zachary.

The tall teacher rose from his desk in the classroom at the end of the hall. With hands clasped behind his back, he strolled to the door, where his third-graders had lined up for recess.

"Kimberly, go to the end of the line," he said. "Stop cutting in. It doesn't matter where you stand in line. We'll all get to the playground at the same time."

Kimberly made a sharp about-face. She stomped to the end of the line and stood there fuming.

"Of *course* it matters where kids are in line," she grumbled. "Kids in front get the best playground balls and dibs on the foursquare court. They take the best seats on the bus! They sit closest to the stage during assemblies!"

She glowered at the twenty-four students standing in front of her.

"If it doesn't matter, why do teachers assign line leaders?" she continued. "Why do they let the quietest kids line up first? Of *course* it's an advantage to stand near the front of the line! Kids who don't take cuts take a cut in the action."

As the teacher opened the classroom door, Kimberly peered forward again. Paul, third from the front, was zipping up his jacket. She checked the teacher and the doorway and then double-checked Paul. Mentally she ran through her "Ways to Take Cuts" list.

"Should I try taking Cut-Corners Cuts?" she asked herself. "No, that wouldn't work. Short Cuts? Nope. I think I'll try Cut-Back Cuts. I have to get the good soccer ball this recess."

Once more Kimberly studied the line, plotting her route. The moment the class started out the door, she stepped sideways. Ducking low, she slipped around the teacher's back and swerved into the line behind Paul. She walked calmly down the hall as if she'd been in fourth place the entire time.

"No cuts, Kimberly!" Hannah called out.

"Get back where you were!" said Myra.

Kimberly only smiled. By now the teacher was out of earshot.

"Advantage Kimberly!" she told herself. "The soccer ball's mine."

And it was.

Treeeeeeeep

Twenty minutes later, the Playground Lady blew her silver whistle to end recess. The students charged toward the school building as they had charged out of it. Each class stood in a line before the door, waiting to be let in.

Kimberly, caught off-guard when the whistle blew, bolted from the soccer field toward the door. By the time she reached the third-grade line, she stood fifteenth from the front.

"What a disaster!" she said. "I won't have time to get a drink before class starts. This calls for Butt Cuts."

Kimberly was standing behind Hannah. After making sure the Playground Lady wasn't looking, she reached down and pinched Hannah on the rear.

Hannah spun around. "Knock it off, Kim!" she shrieked.

As the rest of the line turned to see what happened, Kimberly slipped forward and cut in fourth from the front.

"My cleanest cut yet," she boasted inwardly.

In the hallway, six students stood at the drinking fountain. Kimberly joined the line at the end.

"I'll die of thirst if I don't get water right away," she said to herself. "Should I try Buzz Cuts? No way. And I don't think I can manage Cut-the-Cheese Cuts. I guess I'll try the most daring one of all, Domino Cuts."

Kimberly waited for the fifth-grade boy in front to start slurping water from the fountain. Pretending to look down the hall, she shoved the fourth-grade girl in front of her. The girl stumbled into a second-grader, who bumped a kindergartner, who fell onto a third-grader, who knocked a first-grader, who pushed the fifth-grade boy at the front.

By the time the kids recovered, Kimberly had slunk forward and was standing at the fountain.

"Advantage mine," she said, bowing for a drink.

Back in the classroom at the end of the hall, it was Writer's Workshop time. Kimberly wrote in her journal about a recent trip to Disneyland. It began:

Lines

The lines at Disneyland were torture. I had to wait over an hour to ride Splash Mountain. What a waste of time! I could easily have taken cuts to the front of the line, but my parents wouldn't let me. The line moved slower than babies crawl. You never get far in life if you don't take cuts . . .

Kimberly wrote quickly to make sure she would be done with her story by lunchtime. Students who were finished always got to line up first for lunch.

When the lunch bell rang, the teacher reminded them that it was a pizza day. "Will Myra, the line leader this week, start the line at the door?" he said.

Kimberly cleared her desk to show that her story was done. She sat perfectly still and quiet. The lunch line was the most important line of the day, especially on the days when lunch was pizza. Not only did you get your pick of pizza slices, but you were also guaranteed that the chocolate milk hadn't run out, and you could sit at the best spot at the third-grade table, the one closest to the playground door.

"Hannah can line up," the teacher called out. "Zachary and Tanya next. And look how quietly Matthew is sitting."

Today Kimberly was unlucky. By the time the teacher picked her, she stood tenth from the door.

"A kid can't cut it at school without taking cuts," she

muttered. "I'll be stuck with cardboard pizza, warm white milk, and the seat farthest from the door. Time to take Cut-to-the-Basket Cuts."

"I'm waiting," called the teacher. "We can't leave for lunch until the line is straight and quiet."

Kimberly leaned sideways to inspect the line. Before it became too straight and quiet, she pulled a wad of Kleenex from her pocket. She shot it toward the wastebasket by the door, missing on purpose. Stepping forward, she bent and dropped the tissue into the basket. Still bending, she cut in line between Myra and Hannah. No complaints. Another perfect job.

"All right, class," the tall teacher said. "Have a good lunch."

The line began to march. Kimberly followed Myra out the door and down the hall. On the wall, just before the lunchroom door, hung a portrait of the school's founder, Walter Teach Melon.

The tall teacher had taught his students that this man, more than half a century earlier, built W. T. Melon Elementary School. But the third-graders had heard other stories. Older students told them that W. T. Melon was still alive, living above the classroom at the end of the hall. They said that he had special powers and that throughout the school year he made things "different" in their classroom.

That's what Kimberly was thinking about as she passed the portrait. What else could explain the strange fact that the picture had changed? Usually, she was quite certain, W. T. Melon held a book in one hand and an apple in the other. Now, instead of the apple he was holding a pair of large teacher scissors.

"Hey, look," she said, turning around to tell Hannah. But Hannah wasn't there. In fact, no one was. Kimberly could see all the way down to her classroom, and the hallway was empty. Facing forward again, she found that she now stood last in line.

"Hey, my class cut me!" she said, puzzled. "I went from second in line to last. How's that possible?"

Before taking another step, Kimberly saw that her shoelace was untied. Normally she would never stop in line to tie her shoe—kids behind her would shout at her to get moving. But now that she was last, what difference did it make? Quickly she stooped and tied a bow before joining the third-grade line as it filed into the lunchroom.

Line leader Myra stopped at the tray cart and grabbed a plastic tray. She chose a spoon and a fork and pulled a napkin from the box. Finally she entered the narrow serving room where Miss Treat, the lunch lady, stood ready to serve pizza from behind a long pane of glass.

At the end of the line, Kimberly rocked from side to side. "What a disaster!" she griped. "By the time I get to the front, the pizza triangles will be dried out and shriveled."

Standing on tiptoe, she searched for a place in line to take cuts. Her cut of choice this time: Cut-to-the-Chase Cuts.

Step out! Duck! Step in! Done!

Kimberly now stood behind Paul near the doorway to the serving area. She could see and smell the wheels of pizza behind the glass. She saw Miss Treat slide a stringy, gooey slice onto Myra's tray. Her eyes fixed on the wedge she wanted. She was about to grab a tray when she felt a tap on her shoulder.

Kimberly turned and saw the same thing as before. Nothing. No one stood there. Again she was at the end of the line. To make matters worse, the fourth-grade class had entered the lunchroom. When Kimberly faced forward again, she found that every fourth-grader stood in front of her.

"Hey, no cuts!" she shouted. "You all cut me. Wait your turn!"

Naturally, the fourth-graders ignored the third-grader, and the line crept along with Kimberly at the rear.

"This line is slower than a supermarket checkout line," she muttered. "Slower than a movie ticket line or a line to get ice cream on a hot day."

As she inched forward, Kimberly caught sight of the drinking fountain attached to the wall. Normally she would never leave a line to get water, for fear of losing her place. But what did it matter now? Shrugging, she stepped to the fountain and took a long, cool drink.

Back in line, Kimberly continued shuffling toward the serving area. "Come on! Get moving! If I were in a car, I'd lean on the horn," she said. "I feel Line Rage, and I'm still miles away from the tray cart. Time for the never-fail Cold Cuts."

Kimberly checked the line. *"Ah-chooo!"* she went. Now it was time to make her move.

"I'm just getting a napkin to blow my nose," she said, breezing past the fourth-graders. "Teacher said I could."

She cut in line beside the tray cart. "Yep, the old Cold Cuts works every time," she said to herself.

Lunch tray in hand at last, Kimberly snatched some silverware and entered the serving area. Gliding her tray along the metal rods, she eyed that pizza slice she'd been craving. Four students separated her from Miss Treat. Soon three. Then two. Then she felt another tap on her shoulder.

"No way am I turning around this time," Kimberly told herself. "No one's going to cut me again."

A second tap came. When Kimberly ignored it, she received a pinch on her elbow. Still not reacting, she endured a jab in the back and a blast of breath in her hair.

"I'm not turning," Kimberly vowed. "I'm not losing my spot."

When someone stepped on her heel, however, she whirled around and snarled, "You're history!"

Once more she was talking to empty air. To make matters worse, the fifth-grade class had somehow passed her, and now she was standing at the end of the longest line yet. Kimberly was all the way outside the lunchroom door.

"Well, I give up," she said. "The whole school is taking cuts." She faced the portrait of W. T. Melon, surprised that he held an apple again. "I must settle for being last, even though last one is a rotten egg."

One slow step at a time, Kimberly moved forward. Mr. Leeks, who was sweeping the lunchroom floor with his wide push broom, walked up to her.

"Fancy seeing you at the end of the lunch line, Kimberly," he said. "You're usually right up front."

Kimberly liked Mr. Leeks and was happy to have a chance to talk with him. "I hate being last, Mr. Leeks," she said. "Last always spells disaster. A last chance is scary, making a last stand is hairy, and who wants to be on a last leg or take a last breath?"

The custodian rubbed his raspy chin. "Well now, don't you know, isn't there also a ditty that goes 'Last but not least'?" he said, and continued with his sweeping.

At long last Kimberly reached the serving area. She grabbed a tray and slammed it down on the metal rods. The few remaining pizza triangles looked as if they'd been run over by a school bus.

"And look what I get for being last in line," she muttered. "Leather for lunch."

Miss Treat smiled at Kimberly. "What a surprise to find you at the tail end of the line, Kimberly," she said.

Kimberly stared at her tray. How embarrassing it was to be standing behind everyone! She didn't even know how she got there. Without looking up, she raised her tray to accept some pizza.

"Wait right here, Kimberly," Miss Treat said. "I'll be right back."

The lunch lady hurried to the back of the kitchen. She returned holding a round tray with her large oven mittens. She set a steaming pizza oozing with cheese behind the glass.

"We always save one last fresh pizza for latecomers and teachers," she explained.

Beaming, Kimberly carried her extra-gooey pizza slice to the third-grade table. She was even more delighted to find that Hannah had saved her a seat near the door.

"Well, how about that?" she said to herself as she bit into the pizza. "Being last can have its advantages." She checked the clock. "Now I wonder what might happen if I'm last out to recess."

Anta Claus

"I can't," Alex called from his third-row desk.

"Yes, you can, Alex," said the tall teacher. "Just give it a try." He pointed to the list of rules above the blackboard. "And remember to lower your voice in the classroom."

"But I can't even *try* to do this," said Alex, more loudly.

The teacher turned toward the blackboard. Seeing that the chalk doghouse was smudged, he quickly drew a new one.

"Alex, you can do it. And you can also use a soft voice."

"No matter what voice I use, I still can't do this," Alex muttered to himself.

Winter vacation was a week away. The third-graders were cutting out paper snowflakes to tape on the windows of the classroom at the end of the hall. Outside, real snowflakes had fallen overnight. By morning the snow had turned to gray slush that coated the playground.

"I can't do this," Alex repeated as his paper snowflake fell in pieces onto the floor.

The tall teacher walked to Alex's desk. "Watch, Alex," he said, holding up a sheet of paper. "You fold the paper like this, this, and this. Now you cut the snowflake along the folded edges here, here, and here. Then you spread it apart."

The teacher held up a lacy six-sided snowflake.

"I see that *you* can do it," Alex said. "But I can't."

The tall teacher regarded the scraps on the floor. "Alex, you say 'I can't' whenever you face something new. Perhaps if you start saying 'I can,' you'll start succeeding at school."

"I can't," said Alex.

Meanwhile, the other third-graders busily taped snowflakes to the windows. No two were the same. Some were pointed crosses, some were circles, and some were hexagons cut with extraordinary patterns.

Alex folded his paper just as the teacher had shown him. He cut it exactly as the teacher had. But when he unfolded it, he held a wobbly white blob with a square missing from the middle.

"I can't do this," Alex repeated. "I can't. I can't."

With recess time near, the tall teacher told Alex to tape his blob snowflake to the window. He chose a bare spot behind the guinea pig cage. But as he was applying tape to his flake, something—a dark figure—suddenly appeared on the far side of the glass.

"AAAACK!" Alex screamed.

The figure was a tall, skinny man with a bushy black beard. He wore a fuzzy black suit fringed with white fur, and on his head sat a floppy pointed hat with a white cotton ball attached to its tip. A wide white belt cinched the black suit at the waist. With his red nose pressing against the windowpane, the man scowled at Alex.

"AAAACK!" Alex shouted again.

"Shhh!" went the teacher, writing *Alex* in the doghouse.

"But there's a strange-looking man out there," Alex said. "He's standing at the window!"

The teacher and the other kids peered outside. The only man they saw was Mr. Leeks, who was shoveling slush off the sidewalk.

"Must be your reflection, Alex," the teacher said.

Alex stared at the black-bearded man, and the man frowned back at Alex.

"But my reflection wouldn't have a beard!" Alex muttered, rubbing his chin.

When the tall teacher dismissed the class for recess, Alex stepped cautiously onto the slushy playground. Could the man in the black suit still be out there? Alex stood by the climbing structure, scanning the gray asphalt.

Nearby, Hannah was shuffling her boots through the wet snow to make a maze. "Come and help, Alex," she called out.

"I can't."

Paul slid by on an ice patch. "Give it a try, Alex."

"Can't," Alex said.

"Zip up your coat and buckle your boots, Alex," called the Playground Lady.

"I can't and I can't."

Alex had almost forgotten about the dark figure when a deep voice behind him boomed, "Oh, oh, oh!"

"AAACK!" Alex spun around.

The skinny man stood there. His pointy black hat and his bushy beard flapped in the breeze. Now Alex saw that he also wore shiny white boots and held a canvas sack.

"Oh, oh, oh!" the man repeated. "Oh, oh, oh!"

Alex glanced toward Hannah, Paul, and the Playground Lady.

"No one else on the playground can see or hear me, Alex," the man explained. "Oh, oh, oh! I'm visible only to boys and girls on my Can't List."

"Who are you?" Alex asked.

"I'm Anta Claus of Antarctica. I live in a small, cozy cottage at the cold South Pole."

Alex made a face. "*Anta* Claus? Your name is *Anta* Claus? Could you be related to the other Mr. Claus, the one who lives at the other pole?"

"I believe I am, Alex," Anta said. "But my jolly fat cousin is on the opposite side of the Claus family tree."

Alex's eyes lit up. "So, Anta Claus, do you give things to children too?"

"Oh, oh, oh! Indeed I do," the skinny man said. "I give boys and girls a hard time. I give them lip and I give them the slip. I give children dirty looks and I give them fits. I give airs and earfuls, and I can give them the boot without giving a hoot. But my specialty is giving this."

Here the man reached into his canvas bag. He pulled out a white cookie the size of a pizza and decorated with white sprinkles.

"A giant cookie?" said Alex. "Give me a break."

"This, Alex, is my Up biscuit," Anta Claus said. "Oh, oh! My two trolls, Tis and Twas, baked it back in my Antarctica workshop. This is what I give to all the boys and girls on my Can't List. I give Up."

"So what's a Can't List?"

"Well, Alex, each school year I leave the South Pole in my black sleigh and travel around the world to visit the children who say 'I can't do this' or 'I can't do that' too often."

Alex stared at the huge round biscuit. "But what's the point of giving Up?" he said. "I can't eat all that."

"And I'll give you credit, Alex," said Anta. "When it comes to saying *can't*, you're at the top of my Can't List. That's why I'm spending this entire school day giving Up anytime you need it. Oh, oh, oh! Got to go."

And with that, the skinny man vanished.

Treeeeep! The Playground Lady blew her Bad-News Whistle to end recess.

"I can't believe that guy," Alex said as he trudged inside. "Anta Claus of Antarctica! He can't be for real."

Back in the classroom at the end of the hall, the tall teacher stood at the art table slicing strips of colored paper with a giant paper cutter.

"Now, class, we're going to make a long paper chain," he announced. "We'll drape it around the walls to brighten up our classroom this winter."

The teacher passed out paper strips to each third-grader. He showed them how to glue the strips into rings and loop the rings together to form a chain.

"And after you each make a small chain, join it with your neighbor's chain," he said. "If we work together, we can break the W. T. Melon paper-chain record, two and a half times around this classroom."

Alex stared at the stack of paper slips on his desk. That's when the helpless, hopeless feeling came. That's when he felt overwhelmed by the size of the project. It was too huge, too complicated. He could never complete a paper chain. He didn't even know where to start.

"I can't do this," he said.

The moment he spoke, he heard a booming "Oh, oh, oh!" beside him.

Alex turned to find Anta Claus standing by his desk.

"I'm here to give, Alex," the skinny man said. "I give poor opinions. I give out and I give in. I give the go-around and I give pause."

"Give it to me straight, Anta," Alex said. "How will I ever get through this art project? I can't make a paper chain."

Anta reached into his canvas bag and pulled out his huge Up biscuit. "Oh, oh, oh! So I'll give Up."

Alex made a face. "And you say eating Up will help me?" he said. "But I can't. Look at the size of that thing."

"Oh, oh, oh! You mustn't eat the whole Up at once, Alex. Just a bit at a time. Chew it thoroughly, and then see what you *can* do."

Alex reached out and broke off a small piece of the white biscuit. He placed it in his mouth and chewed. "Yum. Tastes like peppermint."

He picked up a strip of red paper. He looped it into a ring and applied glue to each end. When he pinched the ends together, they stayed stuck. But while he was looping a blue strip through the red ring, the whole chain broke apart.

"I can't do this," he moaned.

Anta Claus held out the cookie. "Oh, oh, oh! Try some more Up and give it your best shot."

After eating a second bit of biscuit, Alex remade the red loop. This time he was able to slip the blue strip through it and make that one into a loop too.

When Alex turned toward Anta for more Up, he found him reading a long paper scroll.

"What's that for?"

"I'm checking my Can't List," Anta explained. "A kindergartner in Kansas just said 'I can't' while trying to do Chinese jump rope. A fifth-grader in France said 'I can't' while reciting a poem, and a first-grader in Florida—oh, oh, oh!—said 'I can't' when asked to spell *can't*. The list is long."

"Well, I can't get past the third loop in my paper chain," said Alex.

Anta held out the Up. "Give it a whirl, bit by bit, one small step at a time," he said.

Alex ate a third Up piece and finished the third loop. With a fourth bit, he added a fourth loop. Bit by bit, strip by strip, loop by loop, the chain grew. To Alex's surprise, his chain was soon as long as his arm. He joined it with Tanya's chain, and together they joined their chain with Louis's.

"I'm doing it, Anta," Alex said. "Just by eating Up."

At that moment the tall teacher dismissed the class for PE. Inside the gym the tumbling mats had been spread out.

"Today we'll practice somersaults," announced the PE teacher.

Alex felt crushed. The thought of trying this complicated tumble had his brain rolling with *I can't I can't I can't*.

His turn came. "I can't do it," he said aloud.

Poof! Anta appeared by his side. Holding out the Up,

Anta said again, "Give it a whirl, bit by bit, one small step at a time."

Alex ate a bit of the biscuit and stood on the end of the mat. "OK, first I'm supposed to squat and place my hands on the mat," he said in his head.

This done, he turned for another piece of Up.

"Second step. Lower my head."

Done, and more Up.

"And now I roll forward."

Alex's somersault was awkward; he rolled off the side of the mat, but he made it around.

"Your Up is working," he told Anta, who was still standing there. "But it's sure filling."

When PE was over and the students were back in the classroom, the tall teacher passed out blank world maps. "For social studies today, class, I want you to label and color in the seven continents."

Alex stared at the empty map. This time, however, he didn't feel overwhelmed. This time, what he felt was an ache in his stomach from all the Up he had eaten.

Holding his belly, Alex looked around for Anta, but in vain. "I couldn't eat another crumb of Up anyway," he groaned. "I think I'm going to throw up Up. Now what can I do?"

He studied the map again. That's when he recalled

Anta's words. "Why don't I give it a whirl," he said. "I'll take it one continent at a time." And with a gray crayon he started to color in Antarctica.

That afternoon during reading, the tall teacher passed out new books. "Read the first story silently," he announced.

Alex flipped through the thick book. His classmates waited for him to call out *I can't*, but that wasn't what happened. Instead, he turned to the first page and began to read. In fact, Alex didn't say *I can't* again for the rest of the day.

Anta Claus did make another appearance, though. Just before the bell rang, Alex heard, "Oh, oh, oh!" and looked out the window. There, flying above the playground, was a black sleigh drawn by eight shaggy black yaks. Anta Claus sat in back waving. He called out words only Alex could hear.

"Oh, oh, oh! I'm Anta Claus of Antarctica. And I'm ready to give. I give bad advice and I give the once-over. I never give a fair shake or . . ."

Suddenly Anta's sleigh vanished and his voice went silent.

Alex grinned. "I'm off Anta's Can't List!" he said too loudly.

The tall teacher shot Alex a look. "But, Alex," he said, spinning toward the blackboard, "you're back in the doghouse."

The Old Gray Chair

Zachary sat in his gray wooden chair in the classroom at the end of the hall. But not for long. The moment the tall teacher turned toward the blackboard, Zack sprang up and walked over to watch a daddy longlegs climb up the window.

"Zachary!" called the tall teacher. He wrote *Zack* in the blackboard doghouse. "Keep your seat in your seat!"

Zack slunk back to his chair and sat down. But not for long.

Up front, the teacher was writing *to, too,* and *two* on the blackboard. "There are three ways to spell this word," he explained.

"That's two too many *to*'s for me," said Zack, and he shot from his chair to feed a lettuce leaf to Miss Nosewiggle, the guinea pig.

"Zachary, stop popping up!" said the tall teacher, adding a check mark next to Zack's name in the doghouse. "Take your seat!"

Zack trudged back

to his chair. "I'd like to take this seat for a long walk," he grumbled. "I've been sitting all morning. I sat during breakfast. I sat on the bus for the ride to school. I sat during reading and writing. I even had to sit in the computer lab. Kids spend more time at school on their bottoms than on their legs."

"Way to go, Sharkey," Alex whispered as Zachary sat down.

"Ol' Zack-in-the-Box Sharkey," said Kimberly.

Zachary didn't mind the nickname Sharkey. Sharks have to keep moving in the water or they die, and that's how Zack felt in his classroom.

Almost at once the squirming started up again. Zachary wiggled and bounced. He swung his legs while rocking back and forth.

"When I grow up I'll get a job without any sitting," he muttered. "I'll be a stand-up comedian or a traffic cop or one of those flag people at highway construction sites who hold stop signs."

Meanwhile, the tall teacher continued with his spelling lesson. "*T-W-O* is the number. *T-O-O* means 'also.'" At this point he caught sight of Zack wandering toward the reading corner. His ears turned tomato red.

"Zachary, do I have to glue you to that chair? Go stand in the hall!"

Zachary headed out the door.

"So long, Sharkey," Kimberly called to him.

For the next fifteen minutes Zack wandered up and

down the hallway. When the recess bell rang, he watched his class file from the room.

The tall teacher stood in the doorway. "Park yourself in your chair, Zachary," he said. "You owe us an entire recess for breaking rule number three, 'Stay in your seat.'"

Zachary entered the empty classroom and sat down in his gray chair. Although his punishment was for not staying seated, he didn't blame the seat. He liked this old chair. It was the only wooden one in the classroom. He liked its sturdy back and its shiny, freshly painted seat. The other classroom chairs, all plastic, bent too easily and had sharp edges. Worst of all, they squeaked at the worst moments.

"I wouldn't trade my chair for any other one in the entire school," Zack said. "I just find it hard to sit still, that's all. Like a shark."

The next thing that happened happened so fast that Zachary wasn't sure what had happened until after it happened. One moment he was slumped in his gray chair staring at his desktop and the next he was sitting on the tile floor staring at the desk's bottom. His chair had lurched and sent him flying.

"An earthquake, maybe?" he asked himself. "But I didn't hear the earthquake alarm."

Dusting off his jeans, Zack stood. He inspected his

chair, running his hand over the seatback, carved with initials still visible under the coat of gray paint. Cautiously, he sat down again.

"Chairs can't move," he said. "Can they?"

No sooner had he spoken than the chair's front legs rose off the floor. The back legs buckled and kicked outward. Zack went airborne again and found himself back on the tiles.

"Incredible!" he exclaimed. "My chair's become an ejection seat!"

At that moment Mr. Leeks came in with his broom. "Happens to the best of them, Sharkey," he said to Zack when he spotted him on the floor.

Zack stood, rubbing his rear. "Best of who?"

"Every rootin' tootin' third-grader who has had that wooden chair in past school years," the custodian explained. "Sooner or later they all end up on the floor. And some of those youngsters, don't you know, were the best chair riders in the West."

Zack looked from Mr. Leeks to his gray chair. "Chair riders?"

"That's right. Why, Leadbottom Billy Keester himself once had that chair, and even *he* couldn't handle her. I'd find Billy sprawled on the floor almost every recess he was kept inside. And now, don't you know, Leadbottom Billy Keester is the number-one chair-riding champion in the entire country."

"Wow, a chair-riding champion!" Zack exclaimed.

"I heard that Billy Keester now rides the wildest chairs in all the major chair rodeos," Mr. Leeks went on. "Rocking chairs, barber chairs, beanbag chairs, high chairs, and his specialty, time-out chairs. But back in third grade, this old wooden chair of yours gave Leadbottom Billy a workout. I bet his initials can still be seen on the seatback."

Zack checked his chair again. "Yeah, carved right here. BK."

"Yep, that old gray chair just ain't what she used to be," said Mr. Leeks. "I suppose you got off on the wrong side of your chair once too often and that's what got her riled up."

"Wrong side?" asked Zack, puzzled. "You mean there's a certain side you should get on and off your classroom chair?"

"You're darn tootin'! All youngsters should know that, Sharkey. Always mount a chair from the left side. Never the right."

"Well, I sure didn't mean to make my chair sore," said Zack. "I like this old gray chair."

"Yep, me too," said the janitor. "I thought of retiring her down in the school basement with the other wooden chairs, but I just couldn't do it. Last summer I gave her a fresh coat of gray paint and put new sliders on her four feet. Old Gray, I call her. Old Gray's the last wooden chair seeing action in this school. They don't make chairs like Old Gray anymore. Those plastic ones break."

"And they squeak," said Zack. "My chair never squeaks. I like my chair . . . but my chair doesn't seem to like *me*."

Mr. Leeks pulled on his chin. "Well, Sharkey, the reason for that is clear. I've seen you wandering around the classroom. I've seen you standing in the hall. Old Gray sees the other students sitting in their chairs and she gets ideas. She thinks she's the boss at this desk."

"You mean my chair thinks she's in charge?" said Zack. "No way. No chair has ever been the boss of me!"

Mr. Leeks looked toward the floor where Zack had fallen. "Well now, that's not how the situation appears."

"Why, I can sit in that old gray chair whenever I want!" Zack insisted.

The janitor rubbed his chin some more. "Then prove it, Sharkey. Come on, show Old Gray who's really the boss around this desk."

Zack placed his hand on the seatback. "No problem," he said, and he sat down from the left side.

Almost at once the chair started to move. It spun a quick three-sixty and tossed Zack to the floor.

Mr. Leeks slapped the knee of his overalls. "Yahoo! You all right, Sharkey? Looks like Old Gray has some kick left in her yet."

Zack crawled away from his chair. "Old Gray is harder to ride than I thought," he sputtered. "But I won't let my chair get the best of me."

"That's the ticket, Sharkey," said Mr. Leeks. "The best thing to do after getting thrown by a chair is to get right back on. But let's do things properly. Yahoo! This classroom hasn't had a chair rodeo in years."

The janitor pushed the classroom desks and chairs into a circle around Zack's desk and the old gray chair.

Zack, hands on hips, stepped around his chair, studying it closely. A cafeteria straw dangled from the side of his mouth.

Mr. Leeks held the chair's seat with one hand and gently rubbed the seatback with the other. "Easy now, girl," he said. "OK, Sharkey, if you're ready to take Old Gray for a real ride, sit down. Careful now. I can tell Old Gray's a bit skittish today."

Zack eased into the wooden seat.

"Stay loose and wrap your feet around the front legs," said Mr. Leeks. "But not too tightly. When she bucks, you want to go with her."

Zack grabbed the front edge of the seat and hooked his ankles behind the front legs. He took a deep breath and gave Mr. Leeks a nod.

"Yahoooo!" the janitor hollered, stepping backward. "Do some chair busting, Sharkey!"

At once the chair's back legs kicked outward and leaped into the air. A foot of space appeared between Zack and the chair seat. The chair slammed down on the tile floor, but Zack managed to hang on.

"Whoa! Wow! Whee!" he called out. "Whoopee!"

Mr. Leeks sat on a desktop in the circle with his feet upon the leg rail. "Yahoo!" he shouted, slapping his knee some more. "That's the way, Sharkey. What a buckaroo! Stay with her, boy. Yahoooo!"

The chair slid side to side, back and forth. White-knuckled, Zack held on. The chair reared on its back legs and rocked forward. Zack saw the classroom walls go up and down. His feet lost their hold, and he went flying off the seat again. This time he landed on the floor belly-down.

Mr. Leeks knelt beside him, slapping his back.

"Good ride, Sharkey. You nearly had her. Old Gray almost broke that time."

Zack pounded the tiles with his fist and rose to his feet. He hadn't gotten hurt, but one sneaker was missing.

Mr. Leeks, seeing that one of the chair's sliders had come off, began hammering it back on like a blacksmith. "Remember to squeeze tight with the knees, Sharkey," he said. "Watch out when Old Gray rears. You don't want her hind legs slipping out from under you."

"Our teacher hates it when we rock back," Zack said.

Mr. Leeks nodded. "Teachers don't understand chairs. Most of them sit in swivel chairs, which have no fight in them at all. Ready to get on again?"

"You bet," Zack said. He grabbed the chair by the back rods as if going to an assembly and shook it. "This time, Old Gray, you're mine," he said. "This time, I'm staying on you."

He set the chair on the floor and quickly sat down.

Old Gray took off at once. She shot forward, halted, and slid backward. She twirled like a top. She rocked from her front legs to her back legs, right legs to left legs.

"Whoa! Wow! Whee!" Zack shouted. "But I—think— I'm going—to be sick."

"Yahoooooo!" cried Mr. Leeks. "Stay with her, Sharkey! She'll tucker out soon."

Still Old Gray bucked. She orbited some more, bounced off the floor, and ricocheted forward. Zack went dizzy as his chair pounded the floor and swirled around. At last, after a final leap in the air, Old Gray slowed. She took Zack on a last ride around the desk corral before coming to a stop behind his desk.

Mr. Leeks slapped his knee. "You did it, Zack!" he cried. "By golly, you tamed Old Gray. That was the best chair ride I've seen in this classroom. Leadbottom Billy Keester never stayed on Old Gray that long."

Zack sat proudly in the chair while the janitor arranged the desks back into rows. The third-graders filed in from recess just as Mr. Leeks left the room. When the tall teacher saw Zack, he grinned.

"Good to see you in your seat, Zachary," he said.

Zack ran his hand along the edge of his chair. "Steady, Old Gray," he said in a low voice. "Easy now, girl."

In fact, Zack stayed seated throughout math and social studies.

"Old Gray, I'm going to stay on you until the afternoon bell rings," he said during Writer's Workshop. "You're my chair, and I'll be on you till the last bell rings at the end of the school year."

Zack did get up once that afternoon. When the class left for PE, Zack knelt by the old gray chair with his scissors in his hand. Under the seat, where it wouldn't scratch the gray paint, he carved a word:

Sharkey

The Test Tester

It was Test Week at W. T. Melon Elementary School, and the students in the classroom at the end of the hall were taking one test after another. On Monday and Tuesday they took the eight-part National Achievement Test. Today, Wednesday, they were taking the six-part State Standardized Test, and tomorrow they would take the four-part School District Skills Test. On Friday the tall teacher would give his weekly spelling test and maybe even announce a pop quiz on the times tables. This meant that all week the third-graders, using number 2 pencils, were filling in oval bubbles, circling T's and F's, and writing short answers, trying not to begin with the word "because."

In the second row, Loren read the seventh question in her test booklet. Scowling, she found the bold 7 on her answer sheet and studied the blue ovals beside it marked A, B, C, and D.

"Eeny, meeny, miny, moe," she said, tapping each bubble

with her pencil point. "Well, I've already filled in lots of A's and B's. Last question I filled in C, so this time I choose D."

Around and around her pencil went inside the oval. Careful not to go outside the blue line, she filled in the D bubble until it was shiny black.

"Filling in bubbles is the only good part of Test Week," Loren said. "Reading a bunch of questions and figuring out a bunch of answers is a total waste of time."

The tall teacher looked up from his desk. "Loren, I hope you're trying your best on these tests. Concentrate. Test scores are important."

"Important?" said Loren. "How important can a sheet of black bubbles be? What do kids get for doing all this extra work anyway? The only thing tests teach us is how to take more tests. I can't wait until Test Week is over so we can get back to learning."

The teacher frowned. "These tests show what you know and what you don't know, Loren."

"But I already know what I know," Loren said. "Tests are nerve-wracking. My neck hurts and my bottom is numb. My fingers ache and my hand is cramped. Why should I try on tests when they are bad for my health?"

"Keep working, Loren," said the teacher. "You have twenty minutes to finish that section."

Loren groaned. Before reading the next question, she looked toward Miss Nosewiggle, the class guinea pig, who was running inside her exercise wheel. "You're lucky,

Miss Nosewiggle," she said. "Guinea pigs don't ever have to take tests."

Loren picked up her pencil. After filling in five more bubbles, she heard a *ding!*, the sound the tall teacher's bell made when the test period was over. But this sound hadn't come from the front of the room. It came from inside Loren's desk.

Curious, she raised her desktop. Next to her glue bottle was something surprising, a red pen. She picked it up and pushed the button on the end.

"Where'd this come from?" she asked herself. "A red pen is for grading tests, not for taking them."

She read the words on the pen's side:

ITS: Iowa Test Site

At that moment the classroom phone near the door chirped. The office used this phone to give the tall teacher important messages. Now Loren watched as her teacher walked over to the phone and picked up the receiver. He spoke a few words, listened for a moment, and then, to Loren's great surprise, held the phone out toward her.

"Loren, it's for you."

Delighted, Loren rose from her seat. Not only did this give her a break from testing, but it was her first-ever call on the classroom phone.

Under the tall teacher's watchful stare, Loren took the phone and held it to her ear. "Hello?"

The phone crackled before a voice said, *"Attention! This is a test."*

It wasn't the secretary's voice or the principal's voice or any office voice that Loren recognized. *"This is a test, only a test!"* It sounded deep and official, as an army sergeant might sound.

"Is someone there?" Loren asked.

"Loren, this is Colonel Cram from ITS, the Iowa Test Site," the voice said through more static. *"Did you receive the pen we sent you?"*

"The red pen? Yes, it was in my desk," said Loren. "But what's it for? What's ITS?"

In a low voice, almost a whisper, Colonel Cram replied, *"Loren, everything I'm about to tell you about ITS is top-secret."*

"It is?" said Loren, growing excited.

"Loren, ITS is a secret facility located under a cornfield in Iowa," the colonel explained. *"ITS is where all of our nation's school tests are stored."*

"It is?" said Loren. "That place must be *huge*!"

The phone crackled some more. "*Affirmative. ITS is miles deep. But the reason I'm calling, Loren, is that ITS is also where our nation's school test testing and exam examining take place. Our ITS officers heard your testimonial about detesting tests, and we have a top-secret test task for you.*"

Loren looked toward the teacher, who sat at his desk, still watching her. "A test task?" she said softly. "For me?"

"*Affirmative,*" Colonel Cram repeated.

"But why me?" asked Loren.

"*Because, Loren, you are a student who questions tests before allowing tests to question you.*"

Loren turned her back toward the teacher's desk. "That's true. I'm always wondering why we take so many tests. So what top-secret test task do you want me to do?"

"*Loren, as you know, this is Test Week in schools across our nation,*" the colonel said. "*Millions of tests, more tests than ever before, are given to students. We must dig the ITS test storeroom deeper every year. Tests are so abundant that our test testers must work overtime.*"

"Test testers? What's a test tester?"

"*The Iowa Test Site Test Testers are four inspectors who travel to each school checking for flawed, fraudulent, or defective tests that might have slipped into a classroom. Our test tester's names, Loren—and again this is top-secret—are Eeny, Meeny, Miny, and Moe.*"

"Eeny, Meeny, Miny, and Moe?" Loren exclaimed. "I was just talking about them!"

"*Many students call out the names Eeny, Meeny, Miny, and Moe during Test Week, Loren,*" said Colonel Cram. "*Unfortunately, this week of all weeks, Moe had to fly to India to catch a tiger by the toe. That's why we especially need your assistance.*"

Again, Loren checked her teacher and met his stare. "So you want me to test the tests I'm taking?" she said into the phone. "Is that what the red pen is for?"

"*Affirmative. After you take each test, Loren, we want you to put a grade in red ink, A+ through F–, in the upper right corner of the first page.*"

"Sounds easy enough," said Loren.

"*For years, Loren, ITS officials have been trying to get a School Test Ban Treaty signed,*" the colonel went on. "*But until that day arrives, our test inspectors have an important mission. Loren, you can be a safeguard against the spread of bad tests in our nation's schools. Think what a disaster it would be if faulty, false, or counterfeit tests were given to students. Can ITS count on you to be our assistant test tester?*"

"I'll do it," Loren announced. "I'll put my tests to the test and examine my exams."

"*Excellent,*" said Colonel Cram. "*Now, one more thing, Loren. Don't talk to anyone about your test-testing mission unless he or she has first given the top-secret pass-phrase.*"

"Top-secret pass-phrase?" said Loren, more excited than ever. "What's the top-secret pass-phrase?"

Static filled the phone, and she listened closely to hear the answer.

"*Testing, one, two, three. Repeat after me. Testing, one, two, three.*"

"Testing, one, two, three," said Loren. "Why, that's what people say into microphones at school assemblies! I had no idea they were all from ITS."

"*Affirmative. Now you must get to work, Inspector Loren,*" said the colonel. "*You must complete as much of the test as you can, as carefully as you can, before the bell rings. Keep your eyes sharp and your number 2 pencils sharp. Over and out.*"

Loren hung up the phone and returned to her desk.

"Everything all right, Loren?" the tall teacher asked.

"Affirmative," Loren said, placing the red pen in her desktop pencil groove. Was all that test talk about the Iowa Test Site for real? she wondered. Well, it had to be real, she concluded. Hadn't she heard it on the official classroom phone?

Loren picked up her pencil and read the next test question.

"Hmm, not a bad question," she said in her head. "Rather easy, though—the answer is C. But the question isn't silly or wordy. It's a paragraph about cows, and although I really don't care about cows, the question is pretty good. So far I give this test a B−."

After filling in the C bubble, Loren read the next question. That, too, she answered while mentally grading the test. Question after question she read, and bubble after bubble she filled in as accurately as she could. By the time she finished the final question she had decided upon a final test grade.

"Not the best test, but not the worst one either," she said to herself. And using the red pen, she wrote C+ in the upper right-hand corner of the first page.

"A fair grade. Good effort. But there's room for improvement. I hope the next test will be better."

Ding! The tall teacher's bell ended the test period.

"Pencils down, class," the teacher called out. "We'll take a short restroom break before our testing resumes."

Loren walked to the window, stretching her arms. "So far the test testing is OK," she told herself. "No fake, funny, or phony test is going to slip by me."

As she stood there, she heard a small voice say, "Testing, one, two, three."

A chill went up Loren's spine.

"Testing, one, two, three," the voice repeated. "In the cage, Loren."

Loren looked toward the guinea pig cage but saw only Miss Nosewiggle, wiggling her nose.

"Did you just talk, Miss Nosewiggle?" she whispered. "Did you just say the secret ITS pass-phrase?"

The guinea pig's mouth quivered the way it did when nibbling on lettuce. But this time words came out. "Indeed I did, Loren. Most classroom pets—the rats, white mice, and guinea pigs—can speak English. We learned your language while serving a term at the Iowa Test Site."

"You can? You did?" Loren stammered. "What do guinea pigs do at ITS?"

Miss Nosewiggle took a sip from her water bottle before answering. "The test animals run through mazes, push buttons, and pull levers—stunts like that—all in the name of testing new tests. And with the megatons of new school tests being produced nowadays, they are kept extremely busy."

"It's true," Loren grumbled. "Kids can't do anything at school without being tested on it. I was tested before I could ride my bike to school or use the computer. I'm tested on books I've read and state capitals I've learned. I was even tested to get into kindergarten."

"This school is lucky to have you as a test watchdog, Loren," said Miss Nosewiggle. "Keep up the good work."

At that moment the tall teacher called out, "OK, class,

take your seats and open your test booklets. I'll read the instructions while you follow along."

Loren returned to her seat and flipped to the next test in her booklet—vocabulary. This test was Loren's favorite. The instructions said to match a given word with its meaning, and Loren was an expert at word meanings.

"Well, Colonel Cram, you picked the right kid to test this test," she said, and began filling in bubbles.

After completing two pages, Loren stopped. "This is a pretty good test," she told herself. "Useful words. Good definitions. It's a B+ so far."

She continued to answer the questions carefully but steadily until she came to the final one, which she had to read twice:

If a room is immense, it is:
A. crowded
B. warm
C. empty
D. purple

Loren bit hard on her number 2 pencil. "'Immense' means 'big,'" she said to herself. "I'm positive. But none of the choices has anything to do with size. Could this test have an error?"

She glanced toward Miss Nosewiggle and then read the question a third time.

"Yes, this test is faulty," she said, reaching for the red

pen. "So there's only one grade it deserves." And in the top right-hand corner of the first page, she wrote F–.

Ding! Test time was over.

"Close your test booklets, class," the tall teacher said. "It's lunchtime. We'll begin testing again right after lunch recess."

Loren stood, rubbing her neck. When the room was empty, she stepped to the guinea pig cage. "I had to give that vocabulary test a failing grade," she said to Miss Nosewiggle. "I'm sure I did the right thing. What will happen now? What will ITS do?"

"ITS has ways of dealing with tests that don't make the grade," the guinea pig replied. "Just keep testing your tests the way you've been doing, Loren. Our nation owes you a big thank-you."

After lunch the third-graders took the math portion of the State Standardized Test. This was Loren's poorest subject, but still she read each question with care, did the figuring on a piece of scratch paper, and filled in each bubble as best she could. She gave the computation section a B, but she found the word-problem section dull and outdated, so she graded it C–.

All afternoon Loren wondered what would happen to the test that she marked with an F–. The *ding!* at the end of the day marked the end of the state tests. The tall teacher collected the test booklets and dismissed the class.

"More testing tomorrow," he announced.

Slowly and stiffly, Loren stood up. She wiggled her

fingers and rubbed her shoulder. On the way to the coat closet she stopped by the guinea pig cage.

"Every joint in my body hurts, and every muscle aches," she said. "If I close my eyes I see little black eggs floating around."

"Just how I felt after a day of testing at ITS," said Miss Nosewiggle. "I suggest taking a warm bath and getting lots of sleep tonight. Test Week is a long way from being over."

Loren hobbled into the coat closet and opened her lunchbox. Four chocolate chip cookies remained from lunch.

"Which should I eat first?" she said. "Eeny, meeny, miny, moe."

"You called?" said a deep voice behind her.

Loren spun around. On the wall she saw the shadow of a man wearing a trench coat and a hat with a brim. She looked all through the closet but couldn't find the man himself, only his shadow.

"Testing, one, two, three," the silhouette said.

"You're from ITS?" Loren whispered.

"Inspector Moe here, Inspector Loren," the dark shape muttered.

"Moe? But I thought you were in India trying to catch a tiger by the toe."

"It hollered, so I had to let it go," Moe said. "I'm here to remove the vocabulary test that you gave an F–."

"Yes, the test had a wrong answer," said Loren. "It's on my teacher's desk. So where will you take it, Moe?"

"Back to the Iowa Test Site, where it will be . . . how can I put this mildly? *Destroyed.* That's what happens to all defective tests."

"And until the School Test Ban Treaty is signed, another test will take its place, I bet," said Loren.

"And I can testify that the new tests will be bigger and more powerful than ever, Inspector Loren," said Moe. "Exams, quizzes, essay tests, oral tests, midterms, finals, SATs, MATs, CATs, SCATs—the proliferation of school

tests in this country is scary. The ITS storeroom, no matter how deep we dig it, is still packed to the roof with tests. There are enough tests in schools to make any kid testy."

"Well, Test Week still seems like a waste of time to me, Moe," said Loren. "But from now on, whenever a test is placed on my desk, I'm taking it with special attention. We test testers must never let a flawed, fraudulent, defective, faulty, false, forged, counterfeit, fake, funny, or phony test slip by."

Freeze Tag

Hannah felt wonderful. Spring was in the air, a spring was in her step, and *spring* was on the spelling test that she'd studied for.

Hannah stood at the window in the classroom at the end of the hall, looking out at the signs of spring. She spun the globe. She touched the bones on the science shelf. She ran her thumb over a pinecone, jabbed a finger in the bird's nest, and pressed her palm on the computer keyboard. Reaching into the guinea pig cage, she stroked Miss Nosewiggle's orange fur and touched her wet nose. After dipping her fingers in the aquarium, she held the conch shell to her ear and heard the *Shhhhhhh!* of a hundred scolding teachers.

At last Hannah headed toward her desk in the fourth row. On the way, she patted Alex on the head, poked Tanya in the armpit, pinched Paul's arm, and pulled Kimberly's bandana. The classroom filled with complaints.

"Cut it out!"

"Don't touch!"

"Paws off, Hannah!"

"Ewww, cooties!"

The tall teacher stood up from his desk. He pointed to the four rules posted above the blackboard.

"Keep your hands to yourself, Hannah," he warned. "That means don't pat, poke, pull, or pinch."

Hannah placed her hands on her desktop. But while the teacher wrote her name in the doghouse, she reached into the aisle and yanked Loren's shoelace.

"Hands to yourself, Hannah," the tall teacher repeated. "Don't tug, tap, touch, or tickle."

Hannah swirled some desktop eraser crumbs with a finger. She didn't know why she liked to touch things; she just did. Her hands needed to keep busy. Nothing seemed real until she touched it. The softness of a sweater, the bumpiness of a plastic ruler, and the coolness of a metal desk bottom were irresistible.

"In school we do hands-on math and hands-on science," Hannah told herself. "That's why I call myself Hands-On Hannah."

Up front, the tall teacher dropped a large block of red clay onto the art table. Holding a length of wire between his hands, he sliced the clay into small cubes.

"Today, class, we'll make clay coil pots," he announced.

Hannah was delighted. She loved molding clay as

much as she loved finger-painting or working with papier-mâché. She liked the cool, tacky touch of clay. She liked to squish the clay between her fingers and punch it with her knuckles.

The moment the tall teacher plopped a clay cube on her desk, Hannah went to work. She pounded the lump into a flat pancake. She peeled off the disk and rolled it into a tube. The tube became a long worm.

"Now I'll roll my clay into the smoothest ball possible," she announced.

As her hand went round and round on the clay, her eyes fell upon Myra, sitting in front of her. A black ant was crawling across Myra's red sweater. Oh, how tempting! Hannah loved the ticklish feel of ant feet flitting across her skin.

"Here, ant!" she said, and she pressed her palm against Myra's back and waited.

Myra leaned forward.

She turned her head until she could see down her back. There was a clay hand-print on her sweater.

"What did you do, Hannah?" she screamed.

The tall teacher stepped to the fourth row. He looked at Myra's back, and his ears glowed red.

"Go wash your hands and sit in the time-out chair, Hannah," he said. "That will be all the clay work for you today. You must learn to keep your hands to yourself."

Hannah sat on the chair in the back corner. She wedged her fingers under her bottom.

"My hands get me in trouble," she said. "So I'll sit on them for the rest of third grade."

But even without leaving the time-out chair, Hannah was soon touching things. She began pulling staples off the bulletin board with her thumbnail and writing words on the steamy windowpane with her pinkie.

"I'm Hands-On Hannah," she said. "I can't help using my hands."

Finally art period was over, and the tall teacher dismissed the class for recess.

"I hope missing art taught you a lesson, Hannah," he said. "Don't grab, grasp, grip, or grapple. Keep your hands to yourself."

Hannah tugged on the teacher's pant leg. "I'll never touch anything in class again as long as I live," she promised.

On her way out to the playground, Hannah went to the coat closet to get her morning snack. At the end of the dark, narrow room sat a battered cardboard box with LOST AND FOUND printed on its side. Whenever the third-graders found something that looked lost, the box was where they dropped it. Hannah often checked the box for interesting things to touch—a fur hat, a pencil case, maybe a fuzzy tennis ball. Now when she peered into the carton, she found something new, along with the baseball cap, black banana, and dirty sock left from yesterday. The new item was a single wool glove, knitted with stripes of every color in the color wheel. When Hannah picked it up, it felt so soft that she couldn't help putting it on.

"I'll wear this rainbow glove out to recess," she said. "It will remind me to keep my hands to myself." Still, before leaving the room, she couldn't resist flipping the light switch off and on.

Out on the playground Hannah was in luck. The third-graders were playing Freeze Tag, her favorite recess game.

Waving her gloved hand in the air, she shouted, "I'm It! I'm It!" And she began running around the asphalt, trying to touch anyone she could.

"Freeze!" she said, slapping Paul on the arm.

Paul stopped with his arms spread like a scarecrow.

"Freeze!" Hannah called, tapping Loren on the shoulder.

Loren went rigid, posed as if sprinting in a race.

Oh, how Hannah loved Freeze Tag! When else could she tag people without anyone complaining? When else could she use her hands all she wanted without getting into trouble? And that colorful glove, so soft and snug on her right hand, made the game even more fun.

"Freeze!" she cried, whacking Zack on the back.

"Freeze!" she said, smacking Myra's thigh.

"Unfreeze," said Tanya, tagging both Zack and Myra.

"Freeze! Freeze! Freeze!" cried Hannah before Zack, Myra, and Tanya could dodge her reach. "I'm Hands-On Hannah! Freeze! Freeze! Freeze! And . . . freeze!"

After ten minutes of nonstop action, Hannah halted. All the Freeze Tag players stood around her in various postures like so many plastic statues.

"Game's over, everyone," she called out. "New game, and I'll be It again."

But what happened next was a surprise. Instead of taking off in all directions, Hannah's classmates remained stiff and still.

"Unfreeze!" she called. "Ready or not, here I come!"

Still no one ran. No one squirmed, scratched, or made a sound.

Hannah frowned. She walked up to Paul, still in his scarecrow stance, and swatted him on the rear.

"Unfreeze," she said.

But Paul didn't budge.

Hannah snapped her fingers in his face.

Paul didn't even blink.

With her bare hand she pinched his arm and pulled a strand of hair. Still nothing; Paul didn't move. Oddly, his arm and hair felt as cold as an ice cube.

Hannah ran up to Loren. "Unfreeze! Unfreeze!" she shouted. She touched Loren's cheek with her gloveless hand and jerked it away. "Loren's a Popsicle, too!" she exclaimed.

Peering into the girl's face, she saw tiny icicles hanging from her eyelashes and frost filling her nostrils.

"Loren is frozen solid!"

Hannah ran up to Tanya and felt her arm. Frozen! She ran up to Alex and touched his ear. Frozen! Zack and Myra were solid as well.

"It's as though my class was put into a freezer!" she said. "They've all turned to ice!"

Hannah rushed to the slide. A first-grade boy stood on the top rung of the ladder. "Freeze!" she said, touching his shoe with her glove.

The boy froze on the spot.

"Freeze!" Hannah said, touching a girl behind him. And she stiffened, too.

Hannah stared at her rainbow-colored glove. She wiggled her fingers. "Whichever kid I touch with this glove turns to ice," she concluded. "It's as if this glove has given me a special power . . . I have the Freeze-Tag Touch!"

Tap! Tap! Tap! Hannah skipped around the playground and touched everyone she passed, and everyone she touched turned instantly to ice. *Tap! Tap!* She patted the kindergartners on the climbing structure. *Tap! Tap! Tap!* She slapped the second-graders playing foursquare, and whacked every fifth-grader on the soccer field. *Tap! Tap!* Soon the playground looked like a video screen with the pause button on.

"Watch out for the Freeze-Tag Touch," Hannah chanted, running up to the Playground Lady.

The woman was about to blow her silver whistle when Hannah touched her hand. The Playground Lady went as stiff as a snowman.

"With the Freeze-Tag Touch I can touch anything and anyone I want," said Hannah, "and no one complains or yells at me."

After she had frozen every single person on the playground, Hannah entered the school. In the hallway she spotted the tall teacher reading the bulletin board. Often she'd wondered how his necktie, thin and black like an exclamation mark, would feel.

"Hands-On Hannah is here," she said, running her bare fingers down the length of the tie while touching his shoulder with the glove.

With an expression of alarm, the tall teacher froze solid.

"I'm Hands-On Hannah with the Freeze-Tag Touch," Hannah cried, skipping into the office. After tapping the principal and the secretary on the head, she raced into the teachers' lounge.

"Hello, teachers. Look at my rainbow glove," she said, shaking hands with everyone in the room. Soon the entire faculty of W. T. Melon Elementary School were chilly statues.

"Don't touch! Hands off! Keep your hands to yourself!" Hannah recited. "Not for me. I want to touch everything in this school that I was forbidden to touch before."

Under the teachers' frosty stares, she touched the large blade on the paper cutter with her bare hand. She placed her palm on the copy-machine glass; she pressed the buttons on the coffee urn. Out in the hallway she fingered the fire-alarm box and ran her hand over the painting of W. T. Melon.

"And there's a zillion things in my classroom I'm dying to feel," Hannah said.

Waltzing into the classroom at the end of the hall, she picked up the teacher's coffee mug. She handled the large "Teacher Only" scissors and tapped the round attention bell. *Ding! Ding!*

"I'm Hands-On Hannah, and I want to touch every gooey, prickly, sticky, or scratchy thing in the whole wide world!" she said.

The bean plants on the science shelf felt rougher than expected. The surfaces of the CDs in the music corner felt smoother. The hairs on her arm stood straight up when she pressed her palm on the computer screen, and her thumb could stay on the lit overhead projector light bulb for only a second.

"Now there's one last thing in the classroom I must touch," Hannah said.

On a shelf by the coat closet stood a silver trophy the shape and size of a watermelon. The engraving on the trophy read:

W. T. Melon Elementary School Field Day Champions

A faded label below the trophy read:

Do Not Touch

"No one's ever been allowed to touch that trophy," Hannah said. "But now Hands-On Hannah can."

Holding out the pointer finger of her bare hand, Hannah stepped toward the silver award. She liked the way her finger's reflection, stretched and distorted, appeared in its shiny sides, so she switched hands. Now her gloved finger reflected in a swirl of colors.

"Don't handle! No touching! Hands off!" Hannah said, inching toward the trophy. "Why not? What are fingers for?"

As Hannah's finger drew nearer to the silver surface, the glove's likeness seemed to advance toward her. Closer and closer she stepped. Nearer and nearer the glove got to the mirrored image.

Then . . . touch.

Finger and reflection met, and a chill ran through Hannah's bones. Pins and needles zipped over her skin. Her limbs stiffened, and her joints hardened.

"Fingers are for touching" were the last words Hannah remembered saying before falling into a deep, dreamy sleep.

Moments later the bell rang to end recess. But the hallway at W. T. Melon Elementary School stayed quiet. The classrooms remained empty.

Minutes passed before Mr. Leeks came strolling up the corridor. He glanced at the frozen tall teacher. Peering out the window, he studied the ice statues of students on the playground.

"I reckon another game of Freeze Tag got out of hand," he said. "Good thing I was down in the boiler room, stoking up the furnace. Soon this hallway will be warm and toasty. I'd better carry the youngsters in here so they can thaw out faster."

The janitor headed toward the playground door. When he passed the classroom at the end of the hall, he spotted Hannah with her rainbow glove pressed against the field-day trophy.

"I should have guessed it was you, Miss Hannah," he said. "You never could keep your hands off things. I have that glove's mate somewhere. Took it off a boy a few years back when I found him frozen against the boys' room mirror."

Mr. Leeks removed Hannah's glove. He lifted her by the waist and carried her into the hall. "You'll have a doozy of a brain-freeze headache after you thaw out, Hannah. But I bet you have learned a chilly lesson. Here at school, hands are for holding pencils and turning pages of books. Use your fingers for the wrong reason once too often, and—*brrrrrrr.*"

Burp, the School Alarm

It was the day of Open House and the classroom at the end of the hall was silent. The third-graders were writing letters of welcome to their parents, who would be in the classroom at 6:30 that evening. Handwriting had to be perfect. No spelling mistakes were allowed, and not one punctuation mark could be out of place.

"Tonight you can show your parents all the things you've done in class during the school year," the tall teacher said.

Paul raised his hand. "Why's it called Open House when it should be called Open School?" he asked.

"Well, I . . . well, I really don't know," said the teacher.

A hand went up in the third row. It belonged to Tanya, a short girl with short black hair who wore khaki shorts and was short of breath.

"Do you have a question about Open House, Tanya?" the teacher asked.

"Alex is chewing gum," Tanya said.

Alex, sitting next to her, immediately swallowed something.

The tall teacher frowned at both of them. "Keep your mind on your writing, Tanya," he said. "Other people's business is not your concern."

Tanya wrote a few more words of her letter before her hand flew up again. "Loren's using pen instead of pencil," she reported.

"Mind your own business, Tanya," the teacher said. "Now, class, if you've finished your letters, clean out your desks. Scrub your desktops, too."

While the third-graders tidied their desks, Tanya's hand shot skyward once more. "Kimberly has fish crackers in her desk," she announced.

The teacher's ears turned red. "Tanya, stop being a busybody!"

Tanya scowled. Busybody was a name she'd heard before. Her classmates had also tagged her with other nicknames—Snitch, Stool Pigeon, Squealer, Rat Fink, and most often Tattletale Tanya.

"Hmph. What's wrong with telling on kids?" Tanya said under her breath. "I just want my classroom to be a safe, problem-free place. No harm in sounding the alarm."

Tanya glanced toward Myra's desk. Myra was tearing out every page in her Writer's Workshop journal that didn't have an A at the top.

Tanya checked the tall teacher's ears. Still red. "I'll just leave a note on his desk about this problem," she said.

Shortly afterward, with permission to use the girls' room, Tanya left the classroom. Out in the hallway she stopped to inspect the Open House artwork the third-graders had tacked to the walls.

"Louis's drawing is a little crooked," she noted. "Loren used permanent ink colors when she wasn't supposed to, and I can tell Zachary traced his picture out of a comic book."

Tanya was about to head for the girls' room when she noticed something new by her classroom door. Beside the red fire-alarm box, a second alarm, this one yellow, hung on the wall. It had the same small glass window, the same handle to pull, and the same words on it:

PULL ONLY IN EMERGENCIES

But four extra words were on the yellow box:

FOR TANYA'S USE ONLY

"My own alarm box!" Tanya exclaimed. "How handy! Maybe this school is beginning to appreciate my efforts to keep my classroom a safe, problem-free place."

Just then Paul charged out of the room. He ran down the hall and into the library.

"I must report this immediately!" Tanya said. She studied the yellow alarm box on the wall and reread the words. "Well, this *is* an emergency! And it says this alarm is for me to use. Time to sound my alarm!"

With both hands Tanya yanked the handle on the yellow box. To her disappointment, nothing happened. No alarm went off; no horn sounded; no bell rang.

"Hmph. My alarm is a dud."

As she spoke, a screeching voice called from the far end of the hall.

"*Burp! Burrrp!* Here I come, Tanya. *Burp!* I'm on my way! *Burrrp!*"

Tanya peered down the corridor. Crawling toward her, advancing along the wall sideways as a gecko might, was a creature about the size of the drinking fountain. The creature looked like a dragon with yellow scales and short yellow wings. *Click, click, click* went its claws on the plaster wall.

"*Burp!* Don't be alarmed, Tanya!" the creature called. "I do kids no harm. *Burrrp!* My job is to keep kids *from* harm. *Burp! Burrrp!*"

The yellow creature stopped an arm's length from Tanya. Its spiked tail swished back and forth.

Tanya leaned sideways to study the thing more closely. It looked harmless enough. In fact, its droopy eyes and sagging snout looked so homely that Tanya almost laughed.

"What are you?" she asked.

"*Burp!* I'm the school alarm. *Burrrp!* Burp, the school alarm, at your service. *Burp! Burp!*"

Tanya wrinkled her nose. "You're called Burp? You're named after the sound kids make after drinking milk too fast?"

"No, that delightful sound was named after me," the thing explained. "*Burp! Burrrrrrrrrrp!*"

"But what do you do, Burp?" asked Tanya. "Why are you crawling around this school?"

"I live on the roof of this school. I sound off whenever someone pulls the alarm. *Burp! Burp!*"

Tanya glanced toward the red alarm next to her yellow one. "So you make the sound we hear during fire drills?" she asked.

"That's me. I make all the alarm sounds," Burp said. "This being California, I make the sound you hear during earthquake drills as well. Every school has an alarm like me living on its roof. Tornado alarms! Flood alarms!

Nighttime burglary alarms! We call out any alarm a school might need."

"But how do you stay alive on our school roof?" Tanya asked. "What do you eat?"

"I snack on the rubber balls that kids kick up there during recess. The red ones are the tastiest. The yellow ones are a bit sour. *Burp! Burrrp!*"

Tanya pointed to her yellow alarm box. "Did you stick my alarm on the wall, Burp?"

The creature nodded its yellow head. A long, slender tongue slid out from between its pointed teeth and shot back in again. "From my rooftop perch I often hear you try to tell your teacher about class problems."

Tanya frowned. "Some kids call that tattling," she said. "But I'm just trying to keep my classroom safe and problem-free."

"*Burrrp!*" went Burp. "Early warnings are important."

"But my teacher never listens," said Tanya. "He just tells me to mind my own business."

"That's why I want to make you an honorary third-grade alarm," said Burp. "*Burp! Burp!* From now on, if you see any problem in your classroom, just pull your yellow alarm and I'll sound off. No one ignores a school alarm."

"An honorary alarm!" said Tanya. "What an honor."

"*Burrrp!* Care to give me a try? How about a trial tattle drill?"

"Not a drill. I have a real emergency," said Tanya. "I just spotted Paul running in the hall."

"Just give me half a minute to return to the roof," said the creature. "*Burp! Burrrp!*"

On its four clawed feet, Burp scurried down the hallway wall sideways and out a window.

After counting to thirty, Tanya pulled the handle of her yellow alarm again. Out of the hallway intercom came a sound, not the regular *beep! beep! beep!* of the fire alarm or the *toot! toot!* of the earthquake alarm, but the sound of a wolf howling.

"*Ow-ooooooooooooo! Ow-ooooooooooooo!*"

To Tanya's delight, her classroom door swung open. The third-graders filed from the room and marched solemnly and silently down the hall and out the door to the playground.

Tanya followed them. She watched her class line up at the regular third-grade drill spot, a white line on the basketball court. The tall teacher began calling roll.

"Matthew?"

"Here!"
"Loren?"
"Here!"
"Zachary?"
"Present!"

Tanya looked up at the school roof. Burp clung to the gutter, jutting out like a stone gargoyle on a cathedral.

When the tall teacher finished roll call, he looked down at Tanya with an eyebrow raised.

"Tanya, the office sent us word about your new tattle alarm. So what's the emergency?"

Tanya grinned with satisfaction. She faced her class and announced, "Attention, everyone! Paul just ran in the hall. Also, we ran out of paper towels by the sink. This morning Matthew ran over Myra's backpack on his bike, and at lunchtime Trish ran away with a spoon. That is all. You may return to our classroom."

In single file, the third-graders marched into the school. Tanya joined the end of the line. No harm in sounding the alarm, she thought as she passed under Burp.

Back in the classroom at the end of the hall, the tall teacher continued with instructions for Open House. "Class, arrange your clay work on the art table and place your shoebox book dioramas in the reading corner," he said. "Some of you also need to finish your PowerPoint presentations on the computer."

But Tanya didn't hear him. She was busy looking for more problems to report. Before long, she raced out to the hall and pulled her alarm handle.

"*Ow-oooooooooooo! Ow-oooooooooooo!*" went Burp.

At once the third-graders rose from their desks and filed out of the room. Out on the playground the tall teacher called the roll again.

"Matthew?"

"Here!"

"Loren?"

"Here!"

"Zachary?"

"Present!"

When roll call was finished, Tanya stood in front of her class again. "Attention, everyone! Someone left the top off the blue paint. There's no drawing paper left on the art shelf, and everyone on the left side of the room was too noisy. Oh, and I spot a jump rope left on the playground. That is all."

This time the third-graders filed off the playground more slowly.

"What a waste of time!" Kimberly grumbled.

"Who cares about that stuff?" Alex complained.

"Tattletale Tanya," muttered Matthew.

Tanya looked toward the gutter where Burp remained in the gargoyle profile. "Hmph," she said. "Who's going to look after class business if I don't?"

The third-graders spent the last hour of the day getting the room ready for Open House. They straightened books on shelves, cleared out the coat closet, and pinned their best stories up on the bulletin board.

"Don't forget to lay your world maps on the social studies table and hang your space mobiles in the science corner," said the tall teacher. "Leave your Writer's Workshop journals and your portfolio folders on your desktops."

But Tanya was still prowling the room looking for problems.

"*Ow-oooooooooooo! Ow-oooooooooooo!*"

Burp kept busy.

"*Ow-oooooooooooo! Ow-oooooooooooo!*"

Out and in, out and in marched the third-graders. They were getting very mad.

"I'm never listening to Tanya again," Hannah snarled.

"Tanya's worse than a tattletale," said Matthew. "She's an entire tattle-*book*."

"*Ow-ooooooooooooo! Ow-ooooooooooooo!*"

Still Burp kept howling.

When dismissal time approached, the tall teacher got up from behind his desk. "Well, class, tonight's the big night. Bring your parents to the room at six-thirty. Don't forget to show them the schoolwork you have on display. Let them read your letter and go through your journal and portfolio. Show them your artwork in the hall and your PowerPoint presentation on the computer. Don't forget your clay pots and social studies projects on the back tables. Your space mobiles and book dioramas also look great back there. And, of course, let your mom and dad inspect your clean desk."

Riiing! The bell rang to end the school day.

"See you at Open House!" said the teacher.

Tanya sat at her desk dumbfounded. What had her teacher just said? Portfolio? Artwork? Projects and presentation? She had none of that ready to show her parents. Even worse, her desk had never been messier.

"Thanks for all your help today, Tanya," the tall teacher called to her.

"But . . . but . . . ," Tanya said.

"But you'd better get going," the teacher told her. "The school bus will be leaving any minute."

Tanya rose from her seat. She grabbed her lunchbox from the coat closet and stepped into the hall. After the last third-grader had left the room, she pulled the handle of her yellow alarm.

Soon Burp came crawling along the wall toward her. "*Burp! Burrrp! Burp! Burrrp!*" it went. "School's over, Tanya. No more alarm business for today."

"What about *my* business?" said Tanya. "Nothing of mine is ready for Open House! My parents will be here and won't see any of my schoolwork. They'll wonder what I've been doing all third grade."

"*Burrrp!*" said Burp. "You did such a good job at minding other kids' business that you forgot to mind your own. *Burp! Burrrp!*"

"Hmph. That's for sure," Tanya said. "I made sure this classroom was problem-free, but I'm the one who ended up with a problem."

She reached up and yanked the yellow alarm off the wall. "From now on, Burp, no more Tattletale Tanya. I'm through looking after other kids. Someone else will have to sound the alarm if there's trouble in my classroom."

"*Ow-oooooooooooo!*" went Burp. "I'll miss having you as an honorary school alarm."

Tanya patted the creature on the snout. "But I'm glad you'll still be up on our school roof, Burp," she said. "You're there to warn us about *real* emergencies. Every once in a while, I'll remember to kick a rubber ball up to you, a red one if I can. I don't want our school alarm to go hungry."

The Sub's Subtraction

Matthew hated math.

This is what he wrote one morning in his Writer's Workshop journal:

Matthew   *May 15*
Down with Subtraction

I hate math. Most of all I hate subtraction. It's also called minus and take-away, but what's the difference? I hate them all. Who needs subtraction? You're supposed to take the bottom number from the top number. But sometimes you can't. Then you have to do a lot of crossing out. That's called borrowing by some teachers and regrouping by others. But no matter what you call it, with all that crossing out, the problem still ends up a big mess.

After putting the last period on his paper, Matthew slammed his pencil onto his desktop.

"I *hate* math," he said, as if to make it final.

Following Writer's Workshop came recess. After recess the third-graders waited in their seats for the tall teacher to return to class. The classroom door opened, but instead of a teacher, they received a strong odor of fish.

"Rub-a-dub-dub. Here comes the sub," a deep voice called from the hallway.

Into the classroom at the end of the hall stepped a man wearing a wet black rain slicker. Bits of seaweed and sea foam ran off his rubber coat onto the floor. From beneath a black sou'wester hat he announced, "I am your sub, and you are my subjects."

The third-graders watched in silence as the substitute removed his coat and hat. This revealed a gray— once white—sailor's uniform and a face half-covered by a frothy white beard.

Standing at attention in front of the tall teacher's desk, the sub said, "Your teacher felt subpar this morning, so I received *the Call*. Subsequently, I sailed my submarine from my subterranean sub base in the subtropics to the closest subway station, and I rode the subway out to this suburb. I'm prepared to teach any subject from subatomic physics to substance abuse."

Paul raised his hand. "You don't look or sound much like a substitute, dude," he said.

"My boy, it's impolite to call your sub 'dude,'" the substitute replied. "Please address me by my proper name, Subdude."

Hannah's hand went up. "Subdude," she said, "our teacher always starts the afternoon by reading us a story."

"We will not be doing things your teacher's way today, young lady," said the substitute. "We'll do things the Sub Way. And we'll start with math. All hands, prepare to subtract subsets to find subtotals."

From the second row came a groan. Matthew had his face buried in his hands. His voice filtered through his fingers. "Not more subtraction, Subdude. I hate subtraction."

"Ahoy, my boy!" Subdude said. "It's fine to submit an opinion, but in a more substantial voice, please."

Matthew looked up, almost in tears. "I can't stand subtraction. Subtraction makes me bored! Bored! Bored!"

"Boy overboard!" the substitute cried.

"I don't get the borrowing stuff," Matthew went on. "Why do they call it borrowing anyway when you never give anything back?"

Hands behind his back, Subdude paced up the center aisle of desks. His fish odor followed him. He stopped at Matthew's desk and looked down with watery gray eyes at the boy.

"A sublime point, my boy," he said. "And as a sub

commander, I never subject my subjects to any subversive subjects."

Matthew's eyes widened. "You mean like subtraction?"

Subdude raised his right hand to his right eyebrow in a sort of salute. "Affirmative," he said. "I hereby command that all subtraction, also called minus, take-away, and finding the difference, be scrubbed from this classroom."

The third-graders exchanged glances. No subtraction sounded great. But what did that mean?

The substitute reached into a pocket of his baggy sailor's pants. He pulled out a bundle of papers and waved it in the air. "Subsequently, here is today's math."

With a flick of his wrist, Subdude spun a math sheet onto Matthew's desktop. Matthew studied it and beamed.

"No subtraction!" he declared. "This paper is minus minus!"

The sub saluted again. "Affirmative, my boy," he said, spinning a math sheet onto each desk in the row. "In fact, I've borrowed all the subtraction in this room."

"Thanks, Subdude," said Matthew. "I'll get to work right away."

As he always did before beginning a math sheet, Matthew counted the problems. "Thirty addition problems," he said. "Addition I understand. Plus is easy."

He began to work. "First add the ones column," he said in his head. "Carry over to the next column and add that. Done. Cinch."

In quick order Matthew worked problem after problem. He was in the middle of the second row before his eyes dropped to the bottom of the page. Something was different. His paper appeared longer. Now it almost reached the edge of his desktop.

"Odd," Matthew said, counting the remaining problems. "I started with thirty problems. I did ten problems. Now look. There are still thirty unfinished problems!"

He completed another row. Again new problems appeared at the bottom of the paper. He tried doing the equations quickly, but the sheet extended just as fast. Now it hung off his desktop.

"At this rate I will never finish my math," he said.

On the next problem Matthew's pencil broke. At the sharpener he stuck his pencil in the proper hole and turned the crank. To his surprise, instead of getting shorter, the pencil grew longer. Matthew kept turning the handle. The pencil grew longer and longer until it reached the length it was when brand-new.

"Odder still," he said. "Nothing gets less in this room. Nothing gets shorter."

Matthew started toward his desk. But when he took a step forward, more strangeness happened. His desk appeared no closer. He took another step, and the desk was still ten feet away. *Step, step, step,* and the distance between Matthew and his desk remained the same.

"And distances in the classroom don't get smaller either," he concluded.

Only by walking backward could Matthew return to his seat. On the way, he knocked four counting cubes off Tanya's desk. He watched in wonder as, halfway to the floor, the cubes reversed direction and returned to the desktop.

"It all adds up," Matthew told himself. He looked toward the substitute, who was sitting at the tall teacher's desk. "When Subdude said he borrowed subtraction from this classroom, that's what he meant. He took away minus! Not only do we have no subtraction problems on our math sheet, but nothing in this room is subtracting!"

Back at his seat, Matthew decided to test his theory by trying an experiment. He placed five nickels on his desktop.

"Matthew has twenty-five cents," he told himself. "If he bought something for ten cents, how much money would he have left?" Matthew picked up two nickels and counted the remaining coins. Under one nickel, he found a dime. "Matthew still has twenty-five cents! Yes, this entire room is minus minus."

In the front of the room, Subdude was eating a sub sandwich. Each time he took a bite from one end, the sandwich grew at the other.

"A class can't subsist on schoolwork alone," the sub called out with his mouth full. "At two o'clock, we'll take a recess break."

Matthew checked the clock. It read 1:50.

"No matter how odd this room has become without subtraction," he told himself, "at least we get a break from it."

After Matthew completed ten more addition problems, the math sheet lay in his lap. Surely ten minutes had passed by now. But when he checked the clock, it still read 1:50.

Matthew slapped his forehead. "I should have guessed. A length of time won't decrease in this room either."

Soon other curious things occurred in the classroom

at the end of the hall. When Matthew felt hot, he fanned himself with a folded spelling test. This only made him hotter. When he tried erasing a mistake on his math paper, the numbers, instead of vanishing, turned darker. The fish in the aquarium seemed to be swimming in place, and Miss Nosewiggle, exercising in her guinea pig wheel, appeared suspended in midair. All this while, the time on the clock stayed the same.

Matthew looked toward his neighbors. Myra was bent over a four-foot-long math sheet, and Peter's paper hung to the floor. They both shot Matthew "you're to blame for this" looks.

Finally, Matthew raised his hand. "Subdude, I surrender," he called out. "Since you borrowed our classroom's subtraction, nothing gets done. Could you return it before we melt from the heat, trip over our math sheets, or faint from exhaustion trying to reach the sink?"

The substitute stood up from the teacher's desk. "Sorry, my boy. Wish I could. But as you said, when you borrow in subtraction you never give it back."

Matthew thought fast. "Except if you don't return our subtraction, the school day will never end," he said.

Subdude took another bite of his sub sandwich.

"And if the school day never ends," Matthew went on, "you'll never leave this suburb on the subway and sail your submarine back to the subterranean sub base in the subtropics."

The sub checked the clock. "A subtle point, my boy.

I do want to be back at my sub base in time for sub grub at the Sub Pub." He raised his hand to his brow. "Very well, as sub commander, I command that subtraction, also called minus, take-away, and finding the difference, be returned to this classroom."

Matthew studied his math sheet. The paper was shrinking.

"If there were twenty-five students in a room and thirteen were girls," he called out, "how many were boys?"

"Twelve," five students shouted at once.

"Correct!" Matthew cried. "Subtraction is back!"

He checked the clock. The minute hand was gliding forward. When it reached 3:00, the end-of-the-school-day bell rang.

Up front, the substitute put on his black rain slicker and sou'wester hat. "It's been sublime, class," he said, marching toward the door. "Rub-a-dub-dub. Good-bye from the sub."

With a final salute, Subdude strode from the room, taking the fish stench with him.

Matthew rose from his seat. He had no problem reaching the coat closet.

"I still hate subtraction," he said as he left the classroom. "But I guess it has its place. Subtraction! You can't get very far without it."